manoomin

A Wild Rice Adventure

Joshua M. Whitebird

IGI Publishing • Minneapolis

To my daughter Lily.

— J. M. W.

Miigwech Harvey for all the help and guidance with the language.

— J. M. W.

Whitebird Books
Cloquet, MN 55720

www.whitebirdbooks.com

Produced by
IGI Publishing
241 First Ave N.
Minneapolis, MN 55401

www.igipublishing.com

ISBN: 978-0-9825503-0-4

Library of Congress Control Number: 2009937320

Manufactured in the United States of America
1 – BP – 10/2009

INTRODUCTION

"Manoomin A Wild Rice Adventure" was created to give children and adults a better understanding of both the culture and language of the Ojibwe People.

HOW THE OJIBWE WORDS WILL APPEAR

The first time an Ojibwe word is used on a page it will be assisted by the English version of the word. If the Ojibwe word appears again on that same page, the english version will be dropped.

HOW TO SAY THE OJIBWE WORDS

Included in this book are two helpful guides that will assist you with the pronouncing of the Ojibwe words. First is the "How to pronounce Ojibwe words" (located on the following page) and the second is the "LANGUAGE BREAKDOWN GUIDE" located at the end of the book.

Miigwech (Thanks)

Joshua M. Whitebird

How to pronounce Ojibwe words

Consonants in the Ojibwe language are pronounced the same as in the English language.

"a" - sounds like the "u" in fun

"aa" - sounds like the "a" in father

"e" - sounds like the "ay" in clay

"i" - sounds like the "i" in hit

"ii" - sounds like the "ee" in meet

"o" - sounds like the "o" in no

"oo" - sounds like the "oo" food

"Zh" - sounds like the "su" in measure

Ojibwe words that are written in plural form will have the (-) symbol followed by the plural ending.
Example: miigwan (feather) and miigwan-ag (feathers)

"Boozhoo (Hello) Warden Willy," says Miika.

"Hello youngster, how ya doing," asks Warden Willy?

"Good!! Papa and I are taking Mino ricing for the first time," tells Miika.

"Great!! You youngsters be careful out there and remember to wear your lifejackets," says Warden Willy.

"We sure will, gigawaabamin miinawaa (see you again) Warden Willy," responds Miika.

"Bye youngsters!!" yells Warden Willy.

bezhig(1)

Before the bawa'am manoominike (wild rice harvest), asemaa (tobacco) is put in the water.

"Why do we put asemaa in the water," asks Mino?

"We put asemaa in the water to ask for calm weather, good harvest of manoomin(wild rice), and for a safe return,"

explains Miika.

After Papa was finished offering asemaa, he had the children get into the jiimaan (canoe).

niizh(2)

"Papa, why do we use small jiimaan-an (canoes) and not big boats for ricing," asks Miika?

"We use jiimaan-an because of the smooth sides and their shape, it causes the least amount of harm to the rice," explains Papa.

"Oh I see!!" says an excited Miika.

Papa then got into the jiimaan and off they went.

"Ok kids, before we start, I want to tell you an Anishinaabeg (Ojibwe) legend," says Papa.

......"One evening Wenaboozhoo returned home from hunting, but he had no game ....As he came towards his fire, there was a zhiishiib (duck) sitting on the edge of his akik (kettle) of boiling water."

"After the zhiishiib flew away, Wenaboozhoo looked into the akik and found manoomin (wild rice) floating upon the water, but he did not know what it was. He ate his supper from the akik, and it was the best soup he had ever tasted."

niiwin (4)

"Later, he followed in the direction the zhiishiib (duck) had taken, and came to a lake full of manoomin (wild rice). He saw all kinds of zhiishiib-ag (ducks) and nika-g (geese) and manoominikeshii (rice hens), and all the other water birds eating the grain. After that, when Wenaboozhoo did not get a waawaashkeshi (deer), he knew where to find food to eat....."

"And that's how the Anishinaabeg (Ojibwe) legend is told," tells Papa.

"Wow!! That was a great story Papa!" says Mino.

"Miigwech! (Thanks!) Mino, are you kids ready to bawa'am (harvest the rice), asks Papa?

"Eya!! (yes)," answers Miika.

"First thing we must do is ina'oodoo (pole the boat to a certain place), where there is manoominikaa (much wild rice),"
                                                                    explains Papa.

"The gaandakii (pole) is what Papa is using to jiime (go by canoe) through the zaaga'igan(lake)," tells Miika.

"That's so cool!!" says an excited Mino.

Miika, Mino and Papa are unaware that they've just passed what appears to be a suspicious  wazhashkwiish (muskrat lodge).

And out from that lodge, jumps three naughty little wazhashk-wag (muskrats) Lenny, Kenny and Benny.

"There they go boys, this time I have a plan to scare them off the lake for good!!" says Kenny.

"And how are we going to do that," asks Lenny?

"Let's just say that it will be JAW dropping!" replies Kenny.

"I don't want to scare anyone, I just want to make sure there is enough food for us to eat," says Benny.

"Don't worry Benny, when it's all over there will be plenty of food for us," laughs Kenny.

niizhwaaswi(7)

Meanwhile back at the jiimaan (canoe), Miika is explaining to Mino the first steps of bawa'am manoominike (harvesting wild rice).

"Ok Mino, we use these sticks called bawa'iganaak-oog (rice knockers) which are used to pull in the rice stalks and knock the kernels into the bottom of the jiimaan," explains Miika.

"That looks like fun!!" says an excited Mino.

"It is, but you want to be very careful you don't knock the manoomin (wild rice) too hard and break the stalk off!!" warns Miika.

ishwaaswi (8)

And just as the kids and Papa finished bawa'am (harvesting) the rice, a frantic Mino yells out to his sister.

"Oh no!!! Look over there Miika, alligators and they're coming towards us," screams Mino.

"No way, that's impossible, alligators don't live in Minnesota," says Miika.

Ready to tell Papa what she and Mino had witnessed, Miika suddenly hears one of the mysterious gators say to the other.

"Hey Lenny, I'm going to go over there and see if they have any food for us to eat."

"Wait a minute, that doesn't sound like a mean old gator," says Miika.

zhaangaswi(9)

What appeared to be a scary old gator was in fact, little ol' Benny the wazhashk (muskrat) dressed up as one.

"Aaniin (Hi) little wazhashk," says Miika.

"Hello, my name is Benny," says a very shy and bashful Benny.

"Benny, what a nice name! I'm Miika and this is my brother Mino and that's Papa at the other end of the jiimaan (canoe)," says Miika.

"It's nice to meet you!! My brothers and I were wondering if you had any food that we could get from you," asks Benny?

"We could give you some of our manoomin(wild rice)," offers Miika.

Just as Miika was about to hand over some rice to Benny and his brothers, a very angry Kenny showed up and began to yell.

midaaswi(10)

"Aahaa, scared you didn't we," yells Kenny?

"A little bit I guess, but I don't understand why you would want to scare us," asks Miika?

"We don't want you taking all of our food and messing up our lake!!" responds Kenny.

"Oh no!! Not us, we bawa'am (harvest) only what we need and no more, and we are both respectful of the zaaga'igan (lake) and the animals that live here," explains Miika.

"I'll take your word for now but remember we will be watching!!" tells Kenny.

Miika smiled and then handed Benny some manoomin (wild rice) for the wazhashk'wag (muskrats) to eat.

"We are finished for today!! Gigawaabamin miinawaa (see you again)," says Miika.

Miika then told Papa that they had enough manoomin in the jiimaan (canoe) and that it was OK to head in.

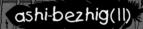

ashi-bezhig (11)

Just as Miika, Mino and Papa arrived on shore they were met by some other curious little visitors, a zhaangweshi (mink), amik (beaver) and a miskwaadesi (painted turtle).

"Boozhoo (Hello) friends, my name is Miika."

"Hello Miika, I'm Bobby the Beaver and this is Mindy the Mink and that's Toots the Turtle over there," tells Bobby.

"We just wanted to stop by and give you a thumbs up for the way that you handled those muskrats," says Mindy.

"Miigwech!! (Thanks!!) Those guys are silly," laughs Miika.

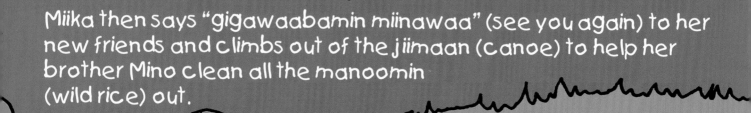

Miika then says "gigawaabamin miinawaa" (see you again) to her new friends and climbs out of the jiimaan (canoe) to help her brother Mino clean all the manoomin (wild rice) out.

ashi-niizh (12)

After a good day of bawa'am manoominike (harvesting wild rice), Papa and the kids were met on shore by gizhaadigewinini (game warden) Willy.

"Boozhoo (Hello) niijii (friend)," says Papa.

"Hello young man, how did you do ricing," asks Warden Willy?

"We have plenty of manoomin (wild rice)," tells Papa.

"Glad to hear that! Well if you need anything else let me know,"
says Warden Willy.

"Miigwech! (Thanks!) Gigawaabamin miinawaa (see you again),"
responds Papa.

As Papa and Warden Willy were talking, Miika was explaining to Mino that once they clean all the manoomin out of the jiimaan (canoe), they have to start processing the manoomin.

ashi-niswi (13)

After cleaning out the jiimaan (canoe) Papa and the kids immediately spread the manoomin (wild rice) out on a blue tarp.

"Remember kids, as soon as the manoomin comes off the zaaga'igan (lake) it must be dried immediately," explains Papa.

"How come Papa," asks Mino?

"Because if you don't spread the manoomin out so it can get some air it will mold very quickly," answers Papa.

"Oh, I see," says Mino.

While the manoomin was drying Papa and the kids picked through it, removing stalks, leaves, and insects from the manoomin.

ashi-niiwin (14)

Now that the manoomin (wild rice) has dried, it's time to begin the next process.

"This process is called gaapizan (parching) and it helps keep the rice good for a long time," explains Papa.

"Word on the tree is that you can talk to us animals!!" says the crazy little misajidamoo (grey squirrel).

"YEP" Laughs Miika.

"Is that why we parch it right away Papa," asks Mino?

"Yep, and it also loosens the hull from the grain and destroys any germs," replies Papa.

"Keep stirring Mino, we don't want to burn the manoomin," says Papa.

ashi-naanan (15)

"What's the next step Miika,"
asks Mino?

"After gaapizan (parching), the rice must be hulled, to remove the chaff, or shell, from the rice kernel,"
answers Miika.

"How come you're wearing those kind of makizin-an (moccasins),"
asks Mino?

"Papa told me to wear these when I niimi (dance) on the manoomin (wild rice), so I don't get hurt by the sharp barbs that are on the hulls," tells Miika.

"Are those sticks so you don't fall,"
asks Mino?

"Yeah, and also so I don't put too much weight on the manoomin," responds Miika.

"Ok Mino, after hulling the manoomin (wild rice) we do the next step which is called winnowing, or fanning, using this nooshkaachinaagan (birch bark tray)," explains Miika.

"Look at all that dust," says Mino.

"With the help of the Noodin (wind) Spirit and a tossing action, the chaff, or shell and dust will blow away and the broken rice will fall on the ground leaving the full rice in the nooshkaachinaagan," tells Miika.

"Then all we have to do is a final cleaning and we're done," asks Mino?

"Eya'(yes)," answers Miika.

"Ha ha ha dusted!!"
laughs the waabooz (rabbit).

ashi-niizhwaaswi (17)

After Winnowing (fanning), Papa, Miika and Mino kneel down and do their final cleaning of the manoomin (wild rice). Miika explains to Mino that before they can bag the manoomin, they must pick through it one more time.

"Well what did you think of bawa'am manoominike (harvesting wild rice) Mino, " asks Papa?

"I had a great time and I sure learned a lot today, I can't wait for next year!!" says an excited Mino.

Finished cleaning, Papa and Miika pour the finished manoomin into the baggy that Mino is holding.

"Now that we have finished, let's go home and I will cook some manoomin for us to wiisini (eat)," tells Papa.

"Hmmmn, that sounds good!!" says Miika and Mino.

ashi-ishwaaswi(18)

LANGUAGE BREAKDOWN GUIDE

WILD RICE RELATED WORDS

manoomin (ma-noo-min) gaapizan (gaa-pi-zan)
zaaga'igan (zaa-ga-i-gan) jiimaan (jii-maan)
bawa'am (ba-wa-am) manoominke (ma-noo-mi-ni-ke)
manoominikaa (ma-noo-mi-ni-kaa) ina'oodoo (ina-oo-doo)
bawa'iganaak-oog (ba-wa-i-gan-naa-koog) jiime (jiime)
nooshkaachinaagan (noosh-kaa-chi-naa-gan)
winnowing (win-no-wing) gaandakii (gaan-da-kii)
jiimaan-an (jii-maan-an) wazhashkwiish (wazh-ashk-wiish)

ANIMAL WORDS

waawaashkeshi (waa-waa-shke-shi) waabooz (waa-booz)
zhaangweshi (zhaan-gwe-shi) nika-g (ni-kag) amik (a-mik)
zhiishiib-ag (zhii-shiib-ag) wazhashk-wag (wa-zhash-kwag)
miskwaadesi (misk-waa-desi) misajidamoo (mis-a-ji-da-moo)
zhiishiib (zhii-shiib) manoominikeshii (ma-no-mi-ni-ke-shii)
wazhashk (wazh-ashk)

NUMBER WORDS

bezhig (be-zhig) niizh (niizh) niswi (ni-swi) niiwin (nii-win)
naanan (naa-nan) ingodwaaswi (ingo-dwaa-swi)
niizhwaaswi (niizh-waa-swi)
ishwaaswi (ish-waa-swi) zhaangaswi (zhaan-ga-swi)
midaaswi (mi-daa-swi) ashi (ashi) niishtana (niish-ta-na)

OTHER WORDS

Anishinaabeg (A-ni-shi-naa-beg) niijii (nii-jii) eya (eya)
gigawaabamin miinawaa (giga-waa-ba-min-mii-na-waa)
makizin-an (ma-ki-zin-an) miigwan (mii-gwan) niimi (nii-mi)
noodin (noo-din) aaniin (aa-niin) wiisini (wii-si-ni) akik (a-kik)
asemaa (a-se-maa) gizhaadigewinini (gi-zhaa-di-ge-wi-ni-ni)
Wenaboozhoo (We-na-boo-zhoo) boozhoo (boo-zhoo)
miigwech (mii-gwech)

niishtana (20)